brb

brb

Spineless Wonders
PO Box 220
STRAWBERRY HILLS
New South Wales, Australia, 2012
shortaustralianstories.com.au

First published by Spineless Wonders 2014
Copyright © Maree Dawes 2014

Cover design by Bettina Kaiser
Typesetting by Heike Krieger | BKA+D
Published by Bronwyn Mehan and assistant publisher Camilla Cripps
Edited by Rhiannon Hall and proofreaders Isla Scott and Luzelle Sotelo

Typeset in Franklin Gothic Book
Printed and bound by Ingram Spark
Be Right Back /Maree Dawes
ISBN 978-1-925052-77-0

Distribution in Australia and New Zealand by New South

A catalogue record for this book is available from the National Library of Australia

For JRS
IRL

brb: Be Right Back

A Verse Novel

MAREE DAWES

Contents

Late at night I watch the words   words of
strangers dance up the screen   too fast to read
I think of smart comments to add   too late
harder than thinking   think then type check for
typing errors   then press send by then the topic
has passed or the person has gone my name is on
the list of chatters I sit here in front of my screen
trying to get a word in unaccustomed to being
tongue-tied butter fingered caught on the back foot
invisible on the list but not in the room
not in the room yet my friend's 14-year-old
daughter can do this she types how r u cool and
c u l8er and that is enough somehow I cannot
say these things and what I do want to say is
too late too long or misspelled I type witty lines
check   for   spelling   check   the   current
conversation   and   then   delete   it's   like
biting my tongue until my mouth is full of

blood are you having fun yet are you having
fun this is supposed to be a relaxing pleasure
this is my birthday present 40 hours a month
on internet are you having fun yet happy
birthday to me I type and delete I watch
closely perhaps there are customs I can learn
to keep my foot out of my mouth and on
the right track   this is how it goes you say
Hey

S S T A A A A R R R B R R R I I I I I G H T
H   U   G   G   G   G   L   L   L   E   S   S   S
or you say

hello room

or you make little smiley faces or sour ones
depending on the mood right I can do this
if a fourteen year-old can do this I can do this
watch me hello room I type nothing happens
… ooohh you need to send … right yes send …
see there on the screen

   Boadicea: hello room
           it's my birthday

I wait there are no replies Starbright is
huggling evita_26 on the couch of sin Ibu and
Cat_woman are discussing postmodernism
there are strings of letters I do not understand
but no one says hello Boadicea happy birthday
perhaps it is the name too prickly too British
I can fix that but not tonight   I can't think of
chat names Boadicea was hard enough I try again

Boadicea: hello room

thousands of people chatting right now and none
of them will talk to me.

I told Caris from work about last night and about my present. She couldn't believe it, he gave you what? Hours on the internet … what about all those internet affairs, isn't he worried you'll run off?

What rot I said fat chance I said I can't get anyone to talk to me let alone goose me, he could have bought me a book for my birthday, but I don't think he'd know which one to choose and he's away so much, I thought he was just being considerate. So Caris I said, what name should I go for and she said willing woman or sexy chick. Caarris! I said what about feminism and she said well what about it?

Caris and I change my profile we are now sexy_chick99   sexy_chick99   enters   the room   we   fight   over   who   we'll   talk   to who   we'll   ignore   willing   chatters   send   us private messages STUD_BOY PMs sexy_chick99 ho sexy_chick99 please cyber send emails send photos we laugh no photos no sex no emails just chat we say the same thing 15 times to different chatters no pictures no sex no home addresses we are invited to little private rooms click yes/no.

I feel sorry for Boadicea no-one talked to Boadicea everyone wants to talk to sexy_chick99 Boadicea has to change her name what about Brazen_Boadicea Bountiful_Boadicea Boadiceas_Breasts.

You need to know this
need to know basis
I am new
I find someone gentle
I ask
quietly in a private room
the meaning of letter strings

my brother told me once
cuntfuckdick
you need to know these words
wankerproslut
these are the meanings
we chanted the words as
we walked round the rabbit traps
fuck, fuck, fuckety fuck

<pre>
me: what is lol?
s/he: a gesture
me: what gesture?
s/he: a gesture like smiling
me: but what does this gesture,
        this lol mean?
s/he: a gesture
</pre>

we are all newbies once
it goes on for a long time
it will go on until I know
all the letter strings
and can make my words
sparkle and writhe
on the screen
changing colours for
each letter
Sea_Spell can do that
I never read her words
I find meaning in
the curve and twinkle
of shape and colour

I see lol
people write it to me
lol lol lol lol lol lol
it is a fireplace
you are hot!
it is a body, arms over head
sinking
        beneath
                the   waves
    waves   waves

help me here
no brotherly fingers
for me to grasp
what is this gesture
this lol?

she told me eventually
I was brave I asked
knowing newbie
would follow
knowing she would say a gesture
(which gesture?)
laughing out loud she said
oh lol! I said
and went on my way
a smug little sister
who found out for herself.

I strip the bed
while it is still warm
from my body
some essence of myself
curls there
sighs down through sheets
solidifies in mattress springs
pull sheets from corners
crush them together
separate the bed
from us
sheets from bed
this is my warmth all mine
you left for work at 4 am
but as I crush the ball
of sheets against my body
I cannot stop my head
my neck sinks forward
and I am full
of the scent of us
together.

Arianne phones me
you are down again she says
I can hear it in your voice
what is it, is it David?

not David, not really
not the kids or the beaches
or the rainy rainy weather
it feels like whingeing
here on the edge of the earth
clear ocean white beaches
it's plenty, more than plenty

it's not enough

there's the newness, not belonging
not wanting the belongingness
on offer
the P&C, watching gymnastics
or cricket with the other mums
it's the mumsiness
and no-one who knew me
before my home filled up
with mismatched Lego bits

I know you, it's me Arianne
I've seen you paint, I've seen you dance all night
and ride the beach roads
from Bunbury to Augusta

well, I won't be doing that again

hey
it's me Arianne I know you

you knew me once
I say
and hang up.

A depression in the landscape

no rhythm in reading
if I can't compare
he reads   Calvino
she reads   Neruda

what joy in reading
without
character slayings
and alternative plotting
with Arianne

can't reach myself
with my own jumbled words
I read sunsets and tea leaves
to foretell brighter days.

In a public room if it gets rough
Jolly_green_giant or
Squashedpumpkinhead
will say lighten up back off

I see the words over and over
Igetthesequence
Ipractice
eyesshuttight
peerthroughhalfclosedlashes
clickignore
changerooms
talktosomeoneelse
talkabouttheweather
rememberthename

whenIseethatname
thatpersonintheroom
Irun
whytakesecondchances
whenthereareroomsfullofopportunities.

The music teacher takes the stage

a bonsai
see how his arm curls
elbow soft
for his hand to grasp
the violin neck

it is hard to watch his joy
such a private thing
he closes his eyes to feel it
I close my eyes so that I do not

I want to be that violin
treasured for
years of experience
seeped into the wood
of my belly

busy busy biscuits
twinkle twinkle cream cakes
we lick our fingers
wash sticky remains
down the sink

I wasn't lonely

oh I wasn't lonely
until I saw his arm
trained to hold a violin neck
propped hand
flexible fingers
truest note.

Starbright: will you
me: I prefer flesh to flesh
Starbright: just imagine
Starbright: I am running my fingers
Starbright: up your thigh
me: I am trying to imagine
me: fingers on my thigh

do I picture his fingers
then the sensation
or disconnect my fingers
give them to Starbright
I shut my eyes to imagine
but I need to watch his words
to see what Starbright
and my fingers
will to do next

Starbright: you have wooed me
                with literary words
Starbright: oozing moisture
                and musk

Starbright: I'm so hot you
                can't imagine how hot
me: I am imagining
                and I am laughing

this is never the right comment
in these kinds of situations.

There are things in my mailbox
I should throw them out
straight into the bin
get rid of clutter
put up one of those signs
NO JUNK MAIL HERE

I think I might miss something
a child hanging onto
grown-up conversation

I should put things into
my filing cabinet
an orderly desk
is an orderly mind

I am better with religious callers
and telemarketers
not today no thanks
hang up
shut the door.

Bacchus2 told me
she had walked Cradle Mountain
she said that I would love it

I wonder if she ever went there
will I ever go?

me:	takes a sip
Big_Bad_Wolf:	drinking coffee still?
me:	it's morning here.
me:	I'm slow
me:	I want to use whole words
me:	or get the apostrophes in the right place

I should close the screen   click
wash the dishes   swish
turn off video   flick
take the kids to the beach   ker-wheee!

in just a minute
I will ask myself the question
are you online too much?

When I talk with Starman27
there is a page of other chat
between each sentence
we could go to a private chat room
let our sentences rub together
but I at least like the jumbleofwords
the way we catch the meaning
even though
fairyfingers enters the room
fairyfingers leaves the room and
Tomtomtomtom2 makes comments
that are turned to stars
by the bad language filter
**** **** ******* ******* ****

we are in a crowded world
this is how we feel close together
it is as though
we look out different sides
of the same building.

I am talking
with new words
with gestures and
curling coloured fonts
I never say hi room
what's the topic
I can lol
I can roflmao (roll on the floor laughing my
arse off)
I know it's not cool to say a/s/l?

when I enter the room
I am hugged
if someone attacks me
I no longer run
I call for L_ancelot
we run them
through
with our swords

when I am tired
I sigh
someone will offer
coffee
a shoulder rub

as if we really are
in our room
snuggling together
planning adventures
setting out the ginger beer
and biscuits

when I am tired
I sigh
I don't want to log off
my head rests
in L_ancelot's lap
my mouth is full
of biscuits and chocolate

I don't want to go
but if I wait too long
I am the last of the crew
last one on board
no-one to hug me goodbye

if I wait too long
I will be on the couch alone
alone with the biscuit crumbs
and the people

who are in our room
when we have all gone home

sometimes late I see another straggler

    me: lots of new people
    she: I'm glad you're here

we don't stay long
it's lonely with all those unknowns
they slide around walls
edge onto our couch

if I kept my eyes open all night
and my gang would stay
I would sleep with open eyes
and have no need for dreams.

Welcome to Yahoo! Chat you are chatting as Boadicea

Boadicea joins the room

Dark:	hugs sweet angel
	I love you
Your_Angel:	hugs you back loves u 2
L_ancelot:	huggles cea
Cool_mint:	anyone read Perfume?
Boadicea:	hi dark and angel
	hugs u 2 r cute!
Xanthus:	who reads cool?
Zeus:	lol we don't read in here
	we chat!
Ziggy:	I have cool, you like it?
Boadicea:	huggles lance
Boadicea:	wow angel, dark, Zeus,
	Tomtom ... hey
Boadicea:	everyone's here Geo!!!
Geo:	hugs cea how r u?
Cool_mint:	pretty gruesome but
	fascinating
	what did you think?

L_ancelot leaves the room

Adamev: anyone read
                The Great Gatsby?
Cool_mint: yeah I liked it
                have you read any
                others of his?
Cool_mint: that sounds like a
                homework assignment
                Adamev
Adamev: can anyone help me?
                Please?
Cool_mint: first you read the book
Ziggy: lol Cool
Boadicea: you still here L_ancey
                babe?
Adamev: oh you lot are heartless
Geo: he left cea
Adamev: it's due tomorrow
L_ancelot joins the room
L_ancelot: oof booted
                couldn't get back in
Geo: wb Lance
Geo: what have you done to
                affront the boot
                goddess!?

Geo: Gatsby is the story of
                   a self-centred
                   shallow consumerist
L_ancelot: thanx Geo
L_ancelot: you here cea?
Adamev: umm thanks
Adamev: I'm not sure that helps
                   Geo. Do you mean
                   Daisy or Gatsby?
                   There must be
                   something else?
Geo: that's all Adamev
                   read it you'll see.

Miss_melissa and Brad_Boy

quiet night children sleep
net friends chat
no-one ruffling feathers or fur
not TR who corners me
suggests foursomes
chooses the players
wants to watch
not kiros.p whom I want to know better
but always sneaks off
old friends
Xx and Xy cuddling in a corner
me and Brad_Boy smooching on a couch
talking about our day
I sit on Brad's lap
we laugh
hug
someone says
get a room
we don't want a room
we're not up to much
the odd smooch
not up to much

but in a room
a PM room
we'd be tongue-tied

what would we say
used to others' words
beading through our own
what would we say?

Helpful Tip:
Want to send a private message to someone?
Double-click on their name and send the
message in the new chat box.

What's in a name Boadicea
a/s/l?
shortly followed by
name?
at first I am disconcerted
by these sly requests
almost startled into
revealing names
my real name hovers
behind my fingers
just waits
for the question
I never give my real name

later
people I know so well
greet everyday
ask me
name?
make a gift of their name
to me
demand reciprocation
think I don't trust them
should I say Ann Mary Jane
Susan Thelma Olivia

petty I think petty
but I hold my name close to my chest
cannot bring myself to
lie with a convenient real name
I deal with quivering lips
but I told you mine!
and close my own
more firmly

now when my fingers type
Boadicea
more quickly than any real name
someone says real name?

I know the answer
I am Boadicea, Dryad, Gwenivver
Miss_melissa, Mille_Feuille …
Boadicea is my name
I am Boadicea.

Soul has a room
Soul invites
I follow eagerly
I know him
Soul is fun
we will have
an edited version
of a public room
all the people I know
we will chat
laugh about Adamev
who will not
have been invited

in the room
Soul and me
what kind of a trap is this
or am I just first at the party

       Dryad: umm hi
       Dryad: isn't this cozy
       Dryad: who else is coming?
       Soul: this is just about you and me
       Soul: isn't it time

I don't want
a PM little chat
a secret word between two
while both of you
are in the main room
on the list of chatters
whispering in the other's ear
secret words
for your eyes only

Soul can be mean
Soul can be depressive
the only people
who get into this room
are those that Soul invites
Soul has invited Dryad-me

      Soul: tell me about your day
      Dryad: I walked on the beach
      Dryad: swam in the cold water
      Dryad: until I was sooo cold
      Dryad:
      Dryad:
      Dryad: Soul are u there?

how do I get out of here
without insulting Soul
or looking scared
or suspicious

        Dryad: umm Soul
        Dryad: one of the kids has woken up
        Dryad: gotta go
        Soul: come back soon cya Cea.

Past weed
>over bare white sand
>>through green blue
>>>tiny ripples

my pale limbs wave
>submerged
>>I move enough
>>>to keep afloat

easier here than in a pool
>I can lie on my back
>>shut my eyes against
>>>afternoon sun

I can paddle upright
>peer down
>>past my breasts
>>>past my toes

through screens of water
>to the bottom
>>I know it is white
>>>I see green

space between
    me and sand
        filled with the surge of tides
           amoebas, fish

crepuscular fanatics crawl
    through this paradise
        as if it were
            an Olympic lane

further out
    whales
        play gravity
          games

I can leap from the pontoon
    hear no word
        no sound but water
          parting at my presence

if I run and jump
    soldier jump
      I can touch the bottom
        then I am caught in float

we all know sharks will take
    those further out
        past the pontoon
            round the moorings

with my ears on the edge of the sea
    and my breath filling me
        with white noise
            I am on no map.

Ignore Abu

I am sure Abu is a construct
made by Yahoo to entrance us
always here
he cannot have
enough other life
to eat
sleep
earn $$ for net connections

when Abu leaves the room
we wonder
what we did
to insult him
were we too petty
are there other friends
he wants more than us?
I followed him once to orgy3

changed my name
so he didn't know that it was me
linga worship and probing
tongues

I didn't stay ...

I create clever traps
tricky questions
look for signs of life
I press ignore Abu
for days on end
but Abu is always there
watching

I think Abu
watches all my words ...
knows all my names
strings them up
connects personas
knows my home address
sees into my heart

knows I have pressed
ignore Abu.

Contemplating the options with a clear head

I'm doing this jobseeker thing
I interview them
try and fill them with hope about jobs
I try and fill myself with hope
about living here
wanting my friends
the kids' friends
wanting my husband here
with me
we moved to the
edge of the world
to be together
and he is at another meeting
or a conference in the city we left
study tours to tin-pot towns
I am tired thinking of it

have an affair says Arianne when I call
you're bored, it happens

husbands always seem brighter in comparison

the web is full of married men
with non-comprehending wives
IRL they are off my list
too complicated
admit it
I'm afraid of being caught out
caught with my fingers in the cookie jar
or someone's fingers in my honey pot

make a space
a time and place
when children sleep
private do not disturb
nothing ever so private as a PM
a new persona

a hint of KY
no foreign cum
I forget it ever happened.

Technology fails
I go to chat

the applet fails to connect
with
the server
my program makes an illegal act
it will be shut down
I have hours to spare
I restart the program
20 times
25 times
how many is too many
more than one

I don't care about it really
I have hours to spare
soon soon it will let me in
favorites > click
Yahoo! Chat > click
Room > click
start chatting > click
wait wait
loading chat applet

instead of chat
diagnosis
terminal unable to connect
with applet

I can email
look at my friends' list
know who is in
while I am out
scowl at the screen
wonder what to do
on another
children sleeping home alone night

here is the answer
although
I do not want to hear it
here is the answer
close down computer purge favorites list
delete profiles and personas
all right all right
I won't try any more
won't waste my time
with a server that won't connect
I'll find something else to do

yes I will
watch me
I can do this
get out the TV guide
ring friends write a letter
sort out the odd socks
Tomtom, Geo
and issacar are
waiting for me
are having fun
without me
I can do this
with a bad grace
for one night
watch me!

I step through the door
there is james

james_the_harper PMs Dryad
        james_the_harper: greetings lady

james does not say a/s/l?
age/sex/location for those who came in late

        james_the_harper: would the lady
                        like a poem?

james_the_harper recites poems
ones I know, ones my mother knows
ones no-one knows except james
poems full of faery worlds and highwaymen
then it is too late to talk with anyone else
with Gallahad or Squashedpumpkinhead
Tomtomtomtom2, cool_dude or slick_wolf

        james_the_harper: lady what would
                        please you?

Christ I almost fall off the chair
used to PM-me cyber-fuck-me

phone-sex-me email-me
what is this
what would please you?

for days and nights
we PM
he poems I read
almost unable to hit return
until I am begging
another poem
a closer touch
I want to give an honest answer
to what would please the lady

one day he does not PM me
he always PMed me
I search the lists
of registered chatters
there is no james_the_harper
he was created just for me

I watch the chat of
other chatters
for james' intonation
a poem he knows

a pleasing undemanding harper
I search the lists
his wings brush across my soul
for days

james_the_harper never was
except for the moon across the purple moor.

This is how it goes, listen now
this is how it is
count the realities one two three
I am mother I am wife
I am friend and daughter
we have read about the burden
too many roles
my family want all these things
but I can be twenty chatline personas too
I can be all these things

until I long for quiet
but then
when I get silence I don't want it
or it goes on for too long.

He: tell me about the sea
she: tell me about the desert
he: you see we are both looking
      for nature reports
she: you want me to check
      the weather update?
he: don't you know it already?
she: have to admit no
she: I'm too busy being out in the weather
she: or minding the children
he: you know I'm not really looking
      for weather reports.
she: no?
he: no
she: then what?
he: I want to hear the day in your words
he: then I know you and the day.

I walk
ankle-deep in waves
between beach and swell

I walk here and know
I must walk to live here
from here the land is up
the sea is up
the surf is up
I hear nothing
over its pounding
I know my lungs
are full of seamoist air
I see wavespray
hang across the islands
my tongue curls
over my lower lip
to taste the sea.

I talk to Thistlehead
Thistlehead in my favorite room
somehow in a scuffle
we are under a bed
the bed with the leopard skin spread
under the bed I am about to bite
his ankle
when he kisses me on
my forehead
a glance
a caress
together under the bed
no one else in the room
not lol
laughing quietly

      Boadicea: my hand
                        under your shirt
      Eloy joins the room
      Persephone joins the room
      Thistlehead: jumps back
                        straightening shirt
      Eloy: hey Perse
                        looks like we
                        interrupted something

Persephone: yeah…..
                   what are u 2 up 2?
Eloy leaves the room
Persephone: enjoy!!!
Persephone leaves the room

he asks me my real name
I should not give out my real name
but do I lie with another cover
or say I do not give my real name?
I am already under the bed
he is stroking my inner forearm
soon I will have my tongue in his mouth
all my names will be his
all my words
before I say them.

Afters

me: I lie in your arms
he: my fingers stroke your back
me: my face nuzzled in against
      the damp skin of your neck
he: feeling your breath cool against my skin
me: surprised to find myself here
he: lol surprised
me: thought we were friends not lovers
he: now we're both
he: my Fermina
me: mmm Florentino?
he: have you done that before?
me: what exactly sweet?
he: you know!
me: giggles ... spell it out!
he: *plaits a red love knot in your tousled hair.*

I have lost years
might as well be seventeen
full of teenage giddiness
I swim in the ocean
stagger against rocks
let the wash pummel me
stand
feel the tides turn
the earth curl
my face pale
I sit and let
waves wash me
against rocks
preferring external
to internal disequilibrium
the waves made me do it
until I am lying half out of the water
bruised legs
sand in every crevice
head whirling
head full of sand
full of cotton wool
hardly a thought left
for Thistlehead
Thistlehead PMs Boadicea

tossed by the sea
or by what happens
in a room
alone
with Thistlehead
the same
giddiness
inability to stand
head full of cotton wool.

Arianne writes, lets me know
gives ultimatums
your line is always busy ...
get a second line ... or a new friend
I'm tired of all that internet chitty chat
I don't give a damn
what you see in Thistlehead ...
get a life ... be alive ...

the busy tone on the phone is no lie
if I talk to her I will be lying

I try to write to her
she has no email
sentences need to be longer
complete with connectors

she doesn't know
I hang myself
over the cliff edge
lean into the breeze
can that salt wind dry tears
blow away internal machinations?

I have some prettypaper
wildflowers on the border
I have my blackinked pen
but it will not form the letters
oh for the disconnected word
a word that stands alone
there can be no such words
between us
at nineteen
I slept all day
cried all night
she caught me back
held me with her words.

This is Indiana's teahouse

here at the
Indian Ocean cityscape
I scoop fluff
from my cappuccino
scoop flecks
from the corner of my mouth
slip finger and foam
into my mouth
warm frothy milk
like the milk
I squirted from the cow's udder
I hated that milk
confused the milk
with other flavours
of the cowbale
hot cowpats
thick cowbreath
dust and chaff and hay

waiting in Indiana's tea house
I look down the list of teas
peppermint

red zinger
chamomile
Russian caravan in Mike's teapot
chippedspout sourmilk
earl grey that bergamot flavour
curdling with milk
or plain and sweet
the colour of Debbie's freckles
as she poured
face pale hair red
Bushells with Matt
who blocked up drains
through three floors
of flats
with pot after pot
of Bushells' dregs
pot after pot
for his lost love
when he moved in
with me
and I realised why
she'd left him

I am in Indiana's teahouse
worlds are spreading out
I can see the ocean
and swimmers
dimensions cascade
from my table
to the horizon
layers solidify
exercisers on the grass
showerers on the bitumen skirt
lines of flesh across the sand
to read to sun to flirt to talk
to walk in the Band-Aid strip
frothed by the waves
gleamflesh forcebreath

in Indiana's teahouse
one bright morning
a computer screen
is one
of many worlds

paddlers
body surfers
castle builders

pylon climbers
ocean swimmers
ships sailing boats
Rottnest lighthouse

I am in Indiana's teahouse
elephants iced tea cane birdcages
colonialism it whispers to me
with its exclusive house rules
to keep out the battered shoeless throng
it takes the best spot
keeps back the hordes
the air itself feels as if
it has been strained
through muslin
in this cool dome
I can gaze across other worlds
sip my iced water
when will she come?

we are in Indiana's teahouse
she tells me of the schism
in her world
the man she thought she knew
but didn't

how she'd lied to herself
until no more lies would come
once the crack was there
in the corner of her mouth
her tongue always found it
a new reality tumbled in

I loved him didn't I
she said, however he liked
it's never enough
I take a sip of her iced tea
and tumble through
with her

she has iced tea
cool sharp
with iceblocks.

Blub lub blub lub
that is the sound of love
the sound of the heart of the foetus
love for the unknown persona
unknown but for the sound of a heartbeat
are there many mothers
who have not felt that love
before the kicks, before the somersaults,
well before the
first cry
blub lub lub = love

for nights I have been hearing
blub lub lub from
Thistlehead
Thistlehead says writes whispers emails
from his heart to mine
encased in words
pulsed electronically
my screen the stethoscope
my words palpating fingers
fingers of words explore the consciousness of
Thistlehead
Thistlehead with the froth of words
Thistlehead with a hand resting on my thigh

waiting for my word, higher more lower stop
PM me Thistlehead, PM me now

I am prowling round the edges of Thistlehead
round and round
blub lub lub
is the sound of love
how many words from Thistlehead
will it take to equal love

I need the recipe for love
from my grandmother from my mother
tape your heartbeat Thistlehead
store it as a wav doc
email me Thistlehead
insert the wav doc in the email
I will hear it
blub lub lub
it will be the sound of love
when I have found the heart beat
I know that it is love
heart through stethoscope or
straight to my ear
as it rests on the chest wall
or pulsing against the neck

under my restless fingers
under my thumb
your heartbeat or mine?

When I'm with Thistlehead
I never want to go
but if he goes first I hate it
goodbye bye bye bye
I want to see his name on the screen
just before I blank it out
I want to see his name
not see
Thistlehead left the room
I never tell him though
don't leave me here alone
be left alone yourself
knowing it's selfish
I can't stop
I can't stay here
alone
no no no
it's too empty
it reminds me
of where I am
when I log off.

Thistlehead PMs Boadicea

he: helllooooo Lizzy
me: mmmm Fitzwilliam hi sweet
he: you are alone?
me: of course alone with you
he: alone at last both here at the same time
me: I run into your open arms
me: sighs
he: fold you in
me: lift my face look into your brown eyes
me: lay my cheek against your shoulder
he: curl your hair behind your ear,
         sssoftly with my fingers
me: how are you love?
he: I'm fine, U?
me: I've been swimming, my hair's still wet…
he: and salty …?
me: laughs … a little I guess
he: gives up self-restraint!!!!
he: I kiss you … open mouth to open mouth
me: uuuuuuumm I kiss you
         slip my tongue inside your mouth

he: cup your breast in my hand
me: curve my hand behind your neck
me: the other hand curves
       round your bum … mmmmmmmm …
he: trail my fingers over your face …
       blow gently in your ear…
       roll your nipple
       between thumb and fingers
me: leans further in … kisses …
       gentle bites on your shoulder…
       trace my tongue across your throat …
me: let my fingers trace across your hips…
       low across your belly …
       grasp your cock …
he: gasp … mmm … love …
       we gonna lie down before my knees
       give way?
me: of course silly! I pull back the
       bed covers … manoeuvre you to the
       edge … lean against you …
       kiss you … lean … until we fall
       together in the bed …
he: oh u r masterful!!!

me: masterful and on top!
me: and now I can kiss you
      and lick you all over …
me: and I start at your throat …
me: … and end with your cock in my mouth
me: … I suck gently just at the head
me: suck and suck
he: moans … and to regain some control
      I slide you sideways onto the bed
      face down … kneel beside you …
      massage your shoulders … good?
me: mm … feeling relaxed …
      do some more of that
he: circle your shoulder …
      circle my thumbs next to your spine
      from the base of your spine slowly…
      up to your neck
me: I lie and love the feel of your hands
      on my body and stretch
he: lie still and enjoy this!
me: I am thinking of your mouth
      as well as your hands
he: circling firmly into your glutes
      and down your thigh

he: kiss the back of your knee
me: melts
he: and the other knee
he: and spreads your legs …
      kneels between them
he: trace my tongue up your thigh
he: push my face into your cunt
me: moans … arches … opens to you
he: circle your clit with my tongue … sucks
he: does it some more … warm tongue …
      you taste of the sea
me: your tongue feels like the sea
      lap lap lap … oooh
he: and as you writhe
he: I draw back
me: I want you babe I'm so wet I could melt
he: I slide my swollen cock
      into you from behind … lean over you
      slip my hands under your breasts
      kiss the back of your neck …
      you feel soooo good
me: moans … can't keep still …
      thrusts hips … circles
he: s..l..o..w..l..y I thrust in and out
      further in each time

        your arse firm against my belly
        your nipples hot in my hands
me: ... moans ...
he: faster
me: feels that hot tension build
        arch my hips back so far
he: Cea ... Cea ... Love
me: let those waves wash over me
me: love oooooooooooohh TH ...
me: ....
he: I cum ... there is so much cum ...
        I hold you so tightly
he: ....
me: mmmmmmmmmm
he: love ...?
me: mm?
he: I roll onto my side
        pull you in against me face to face
me: so warm so wet so ... loved
me: kiss your mouth
he: kiss you back gently
he: trace your chin line
me: everything else fades when I am with you
he: what else is there
        but you and me together!

me: snuggles
he: stroke your back
me: pull the blankets up it's getting cold
      and I have to go soon …
he: how soon?
me: 5 minutes … sorry …
me: love let's hold hands and go together
he: first another kiss
me: let's make another time
he: holds you so closely I feel all your ribs
he: next Tuesday at our Tuesday time?
me: if I can wait that long
he: you'll mail me
me: you know I will
he: we're holding hands
me: on the count of three
he: bye love …
me: bye …

I send him *a poem from the time of the pharaohs*

With you here at Mertu
is like being at Heliopolis already.

We return to the tree-filled garden
my arms full of flowers
    my fingers full of words for you
    just waiting to be typed.

Looking at my reflection in the still pool –
my arms full of flowers –
    see me in the pool with flowers
    talking to you is like
    whispering to my reflection
    I know you are here
    I twirl in the room
    chat with friends
    know your eyes are on me.

I see you creeping on tip-toe
to kiss me from behind

my hair heavy with perfume
     with your words in my ear and
your arms around me
I feel as if I belong to the Pharaoh.

So small are the flowers of Seamu
whoever looks at them feels a giant
     so brief the words we exchange
     how overwhelming the feelings
     oh that I could be
first among your loves
like a freshly sprinkled garden of grass and
perfumed flowers.

Pleasant is the channel you have dug
in the freshness of the north wind
     I am caught in tendrils
     of the passion flower
     tenuous across time zones
     continents
     cultures
tranquil our paths when we find
     each other for an unexpected hour
when your hand rests in mine in joy.

Your voice gives life, like nectar
>to see your name on the screen
>I have whiled away many hours
to see you is more than food or drink.

There are flowers of Zait in the garden
I cut and bind flowers for you
making a garland
>I search out words
>record my days
>send them to you
>any way I can
and when you get drunk
and lie down to sleep it off
I am the one who bathes the dust from your feet
>well I would if I could
>if you were here or I was there
>if I washed dust from anyone's feet at all.*

I find my love fishing
his feet in the shallows
>I always preferred swimming
>to fishing
>come swim my love

then
we   shall
have breakfast
together
drink beer.

    With the magic of my words
I *offer him my thighs*
he is caught in the spell
    of his own weaving.

                Anonymous 1567-1085 BC
                Boadicea 3rd millennium AD

Another poem that melts
another note of leaving
only thirty days you say
but I am never here
never logged on
to receive your goodbyes
I come to them late
when the sheets are cold
the ink has dried
send and receive
internet mail
your message emerges
tells me you left six hours ago
my fingers fly a reply
as if it's possible
to go back six hours
my message crosses
time zones in seconds
go back six hours
go back
thirty days it might as well
be forever
I'll shut down my connection
give up chat
you know I only ever come here for you.

I'll kiss you yes I will
if you'll come back
do anything you want
hold my heart out to you
in the palms of my hands

thirty days and thirty nights
it's a long time in chat
Thistlehead
years of existence not days
there are temptations

I have divided flesh and electronic
mediums
snip snap
but within one?
climb numb-limbed from one bed
to another and back
without a sigh or guilty look
I've never been good at that

but without you
I can do it now in cyber
another space
a new persona

push out my worlds
make my rooms
cybersexpartner1 cybersexpartner2 …

I will never
send send send
this to Thistlehead
no one likes to be told
they are on the list
on the list but
not on the top of it.

An hour's dalliance

easy to be me
easy to please
please to ease
your pleasure your joy
adore me
I am all you want
for an hour I can be
the me I want to be or
the you you want me to be
which is the same thing
for an hour
I can lol at your jokes
no need to say you're gorgeous except
your habit of picking your teeth at the table
or that Brut aftershave …

you're gorgeous
you go to my head
I wish you were here
if wishes were horses
I'd ride you
here in my house in the flesh …

you: gasp
you: here is my email
you: get ICQ, real time
you: call me
you: put me on your friends' list
you: find me next Sunday
you: here is my real name
you: I want you
you: I need you
you: I love you

I saunter from the room
with a heated backward glance
I change my name
with no regrets.

If you have a partner a spouse a girl/boyfriend
a significant other do you want all of them all
their personas, love them all want them all and
if you do really do right in the guts of it not just
there right on that happy happy lovey lovey
surface if you do want and love all of them do
you ever wonder if this is too much to ask that
all your partner's selves 1, 2, 3 ... that in each
of them a portion big or small should be
reserved for loving you that downtown in the
office the wheeler-dealer spouse squeezing deals
should be feeling a
squeeze in their heart for you
not since Copernicus has there been a
heavens-move-around-me jaunt
I am tired of all my voices
I love my different selves
but I am tired of wanting
everything
to fulfill all of my wants to be all I can be
am I out of control?
would you on another spouse away
children sleeping
horny night
tell me would you

could you
if you were me
and Gallahad
was in the room
shiny Gallahad
with his silvered words if
he was in the room
PMed you and
there you are the two of you
he slides his fingers
between your thighs
do you stamp your foot
press ignore
stamp your foot
say no
stamp your foot
say don't stop
no-one will ever know
no death diseases to catch
you your conscience and Gallahad
those warm fingers
open the flower
petals of your vulva
you stamp your foot …

I know you will not vanish
will not change your name
you are there
every day
every night
except Sunday when you swim
will you speak to me
answer my hellos
include me in the conversation
meet me in our small white room
or press ignore
pretend that you have never
seen my pale body
flit across the face
of white walls
nipples and lips
never kissed
stroked
loved
can I bear it if you press ignore
fill the chat room with your presence
every hour I am there
and never speak to me
I can imagine myself
in front of the whole room

calling you down
naming our actions
saying age sex time action location
don't pretend it never happened
it was a dream of a fuck
wasn't it?

Dryad and Thor_the_barbarian

Thor is like a moth
at my window
through glass
scraps of organza
a whirling invitation

lured out
my eyes focus
on stars
wings of Thor
merge black

I stumble
in this quiet place
do I feel
a beating of wings
or the useless beat
of my fingers
on the keys
in the night?

How far back
does he mean to go
back to when
we first met
to some still time
when things were perfect
choose he says
one or the other
but I can be wife
mother, daughter
friend, colleague, worker
I can be all these things
he wants me to be
all these things
it is Boadicea, Dryad
Miss_melissa, enfanta …
he has a problem with

can't see a way out
once a wife … always a wife
or an ex-wife or a widow
watch me cast off these names
like I cast off my clothes
for Gallahad

watch
I can loll in the sea
let salt and iodine seep
into my mucus membranes
waves wash over me
I must jump
over
            or
                        dive
                                    under
keeping my distance
from the shore
I bob in waves.

There are questions
you need to find answers for
questions someone will ask in a crowded room
questions you will ask yourself
in unguarded moments
Is cybersex adultery?
Do women really cum when they cyber?
How do you know you're addicted to chat?
Do chat love affairs ever work IRL?
How do I appease the Yahoo boot goddess?
How do I know you're really you?
Are you like this IRL?
Is there a God?
How do I know it's really you in the photograph?
What is your real name?
Why are you here?
How do I know I'm a fantastic cyberlover?
Why do you girls all kiss and huggle
and smooch each other when you meet in here?
How do you choose a cybersex partner?
How many angels can twirl
on the head of a pin?
How many simultaneous cybers
can a chat goddess have?

If you want answers
you need to go there
create personas
remember your password
log in
get a chat-honey
find out for yourself
is it adultery
does cyber matter
in the scheme of things
in matters of the heart
no more than a wank …
less than a wank
just like phone sex

if it isn't real
isn't sex
doesn't count …
you can be
a cyber virgin
every time.

You must give it all up he says
I say nothing at all
perhaps I can give up Dragon and Ibu
or Tomtomtomtom2
but what about Mille_Feuille
Miss_melissa, Dryad and enfanta
who will I be
if I am not Boadicea?

you must give it all up she says
when she catches me being Miss_melissa
I'm feeling so flirty
I'm being Miss_melissa I say
you haven't a flirty bone in your body she says
get a life
forget Miss_melissa, Tomtom and
that Thistlehead

I think of Thistlehead and Boadicea
Mille_Feuille and Dragon_tips
Dryad and Thor_the_barbarian
Miss_melissa and Brad_Boy
enfant_terrible and just_jack
if I snip out my Mille_Feuille persona
Dragon_tips goes too

none of the others will
talk to Dragon
all that scary hot breath
I think of them
two by two
saying goodbye
me it will be up to me
saying goodbye

  Miss_melissa: bye Brad huggles
  Brad_Boy: bye Lissy smooches
       see you soooon
  Miss_melissa: won't be
       coming back Brad
  Miss_melissa: I'm as good
       as dead Brad
  Brad_Boy: what Lissy,
       what's going on Lissy
  Miss_melissa leaves the room
  Brad_Boy: Lissy, come back Lissy
  Miss_melissa is unavailable just now

this will be me
a different me
but still me
saying goodbye over and over.

How to indulge in Simultaneous cybersex with the help of Control+C and Control+V

Dragon-tips PMs Mille_Feuille
he:	Mille darling
she:	hi sweet
he:	how was your day?
she:	throw myself into your arms
he:	are you going to be on line for a while
he:	or are you just getting emails

just_jack PMs enfant_terrible
he:	we meet again you hot thing you
she:	hi sweet
she:	lean forward brush your lower lip with my tongue
she:	throw myself into your arms
he:	love the feel of your breasts
he:	against my naked chest

Tomtomtomtom2 PMs Boadicea
    he: I've been looking
               everywhere for you
    she: hi sweet
    she: huggles
    he: u r on the screen
               but never in the room
                 – some hot pm?
    she: u know I only ever think of TH
    she: but he is not here

Brad_Boy PMs Miss_melissa
    he: long time you hot babe
    she: hi sweet
    he: what's your time frame Lissy
    she: throw myself into your arms
    she: brush your lower lip
               with my tongue
    he: hmm so this is going to be quick?
    she: love the feel of my breasts
               against your skin

Insouciance
you warned me
said the word
defined it as loss of mind
loss of soul
I laughed
lack of concern
sounds good for awhile

days have gone
I am limp
I rerun your words
my words
endless cycles
let my body re experience
care for nothing but
an elliptical pattern
in a bright white room
your fingers firm against my neck

once I looked for signs of life in others
now I find no signs of life in myself
waves of light and sound
feather against my skin
memories scratching in.

I can end this any time I want
watch me
I call my server
I say cut my time
to 5 hours a week

he says it'll cost you more
you gotta good deal

I say cut my time to five hours
well it has to be in writing

I'll think about it I say.

I go to the city
days are hot
I throw my heated body
into waves
waves that are cluttered
boards and bodies
water that is murky
I walk on wet sand
my footfalls in footprints
at home
the sea is clear
uncrowded
so cold
my body
disappears.

It has to end somewhere
there will be tears before bedtime
yes there will
if you keep on …
if you don't stop …

you've got to
got to give up chat
he says
and when I say
if you give up overtime
I know I've got him
although he wiggles a bit with
but I only do it for the family …
you like the extra money …

five hours he says
I could drop overtime
to five hours

me too
I can live
within
five hours chat
if I have to

you must be faithful he says
I say U 2

decide he says

how can I decide
have I made love with him
felt his tongue inside my mouth
and thought his name
no
our jumble of limbs
the tangle of my thoughts
are tumbled through
the veils of Thistlehead's words
I can't decide I say
when will you he says
he stands to walk away
I catch his hand
tip the balance
I say
tip the balance
I press my lips
against
his mouth
the nowords space

between a kiss
and the absence
of response.

                me: 4 am
                me: ease under sheet

he rolls over grabs my breast, kisses my mouth
smoothes my waist

        me: stop
        me: wait
        me: back off
        me: you have to tell me
                what you are doing
        me: I need to know
        me   first the words
        me: then the touch

        me: these unplanned caresses
        me: are too much
        me: like this
        me: I scratch my fingers slowly
        me: down your spine
        me: my fingers continue
        me: to the cleft between
                your buttocks

me: through that tight
         smooth place
me: your skin is so soft
me: your bum is so tight
me: my fingers are like oil

oh forget it he says, I want to make love
not lyric poems, it's 4 am go back to sleep

me: my feet make
me: little angry kicks
me: against each other
me: against the sheet
me: kick kick kick.

There is nothing wrong with me

see me at work efficient patient
reports written desk tidied
see me at home bread baked
children grown garden weeded
birthday presents sent
to the right person on the right date
I kiss you don't I
lips to lips
ask about your day
I swim up and down the pool
my heart rate reaches 140 bpm
I recover quickly
moles checked annually
vision biannually
if you ask me again what is wrong
I will snap snappity snap
then you will tell me
I have a problem with anger!

Conan_the_barbarian PMs Gwenivver

<pre>
Gwenivver: I cum
Gwenivver: my hair flared out
Gwenivver: across the pillow
Gwenivver: oooooooooohh
Gwenivver: ....
</pre>

I am glazed
plastered against the sheets
mesmerised by love words

<pre>
Gwenivver: I stretch
                  mmmmmmmmmmm
Conan_the_barbarian:I hold the knife
Conan_the_barbarian:I have slipped
Conan_the_barbarian:from beneath the pillow
Conan_the_barbarian:against your throat
Conan_the_barbarian:I press the sharp blade
Conan_the_barbarian:against your damp skin
</pre>

I call for L_ancelot
but even he can't reach me here
I know what to do next if my fingers will move

neurons reconnect
I press close press ignore
I scream for L_ancelot
but not before
I feel first
blood
swell
at knife's
e
d
g
e.

To: Thistlehead@hotmail.com
From: Boadicea@hotmail.com
Subject: forgetting is so long

I scythe through my life for a bundle of days
to gather and bind and send to you

but with no replies words are chaff in my mouth
and instead of a harvest it feels like a frost

so with this last letter I send you my love
curled up the ribbon you wove
through my hair.

My fingers type
they type out my
internet ID
my password
even if my mind forgets
my fingers remember the pattern
*****

my fingers know all the sequences
bankcard number
eftpos number
too many phone numbers
my fingers can find
that knotty place
on your left shoulder
without sight
without hearing
I know about you
let my fingers trace
lace us together

rope you in
tie you down
let my fingers circle
the knot in your shoulder
learn the names of

bones and muscles
clavicle scapular trapezius
vertebrae deltoid infraspinatus
this is what we are made of
smooth muscles
well oiled
exercised
with a knotty centre
a hunched shoulder
what made it
that burl in the smooth flow of flesh.

Welcome to Yahoo! Chat you are chatting as Boadicea

Boadicea enters the room
Dark enters the room

Your_Angel:	Dark baby …
L_ancelot:	huggles cea
Boadicea:	hi dark and angel hugs
Boadicea:	things good with you?
Boadicea:	huggles Lancey … you seen TH?
Boadicea:	anyone seen Thistlehead
Xanthus:	I think he went to war
Adamev:	wtf really maybe I haven't seen him since about then
Zeus:	I come in here to get away from that stuff
Boadicea:	wow it's the whole gang again
Boadicea:	everyone's here tomtomtom!!! Still no TH
Dark:	things good
Your_Angel:	with us

L_ancelot: no cea haven't seen him
                  thought you guys were
                  in contact IRL
Adamev: does anyone know
                  anyone who's in the
                  conflict?
Cool_mint: what do you think
                  about the war
Cool_mint: would you go?
Zeus: oh shut up this is
                  books and literature
Zeus: and yes that covers
                  war and peace …
                  but not this war
Strandwolf: hello room
Boadicea: sniffle
                  no I can't find him
Cool_mint: but surely you
                  think it's important
Geo: press ignore folks
L_ancelot: you tried his
                  other names
L_ancelot: and what have
                  you been doing
L_ancelot: online - not in the

                        main room - not
                        with TH!?
        L_ancelot: what have
                        you been doing?
Geo leaves the room
Geo joins the room
        Strandwolf: hello room
        Boadicea: u know I am
                        always online
        L_ancelot: yes but what have
                        you been doing
        Boadicea: not sure I want
                        to answer that
        Adamev: can make some fairly
                        accurate guesses
                        about that
        Adamev: anyone else care to guess
        Geo: would never kiss and
                        tell huh cea?

He ropes me up leaves me screaming
a week later when we meet
my limbs will be cramped and shaking
I will have to beg him to release me

with my tears I slip the ropes
find my knife where it has fallen
he will remake the room and find me here

I am Boadicea there will be blood.

Thistlehead PMs Boadicea

Thistlehead:	are you here
Thistlehead:	please be here
Thistlehead:	I need you here
Thistlehead:	I'm sorry I've been gone
Thistlehead:	can u imagine
	how I've wanted you
Boadicea:	sniffle
Thistlehead:	Penelope you are here!
Thistlehead:	and I grab onto you
Thistlehead:	as if you are
Thistlehead:	that last
Thistlehead:	unstained person
Thistlehead:	?
Thistlehead:	?
Thistlehead:	you there Penelope?
Boadicea:	sniffle
Thistlehead:	I'm sorry so sorry
Boadicea:	Odysseus.

Boadicea has mail from Thistlehead

today I got email
email from Thistlehead
wav docs
my favorite
it's words
words in his mouth
recorded
he does it just for me
today's is different
my words my voice my recording
interwoven with his words his voice
my words his voice
words crinkle like cellophane
I can hold them in my fingers
moisture dissolves them like rice paper
I wasn't lonely
oh I wasn't lonely
my voice his words
somewhere we are together
somewhere our worlds
hang so closely together
that he can end the sentence I begin.

He says read it
read the article in *The Australian* on page 5
Wednesday's
it's in the lounge, shall I get it for you?
I say give me a chance
a chance to read
to understand
to switch off chat
make the words flow
smoothly from my mouth
into the air
across space to nuzzle
into your ear canals
and little hammer bones
stop my fingers
tapping out
a sign for smiley face
while my flesh mouth
is down down down

I am in a corner
on the edge
if I could
say one sentence
without a line break

I know he would
believe me
my fingers will not stop
tapping
my words will
not go together
his face
his voice
I cannot hear his words
I am so full of his face.

Ziggy: anyone for a renga
Boadicea: who's in?
Xanthus: let's get down to it
Xanthus: anyone not in shut up
Xanthus: outside my window
Xanthus: leaf litter overfills street
Xanthus: my heart feels a chill
Ziggy: September Mango
Ziggy: too early
                astringent flesh
Ziggy: my open mouthed smile
Boadicea: mimosa, wattle
Boadicea: we stretch words
                though hemispheres
Boadicea: nos jolies saisons
Thistlehead: the seasons though fine
Thistlehead: cannot compare
                to my love's
Thistlehead: visage enchantée
Thistlehead: her moods are mercurial
Thistlehead: her hair is whipped
                in night winds
Xanthus: trying to break
                all the rules at once?
Boadicea: your meaning is plain

Boadicea: no tanka only English
Boadicea: stiff words dead leaves
                 merde!

Truth or dare

I let him fuck me under the open sky
with my back to granite
grinding the hard stars of my bones
into rock
softhard hardsoft
airrock boneflesh
he's always wanted to do that
outside, open sky
someone will see us
hear us
find traces, secretions
trickling through lichen
I hit the pleasure trail
let my fingers type out
against rock
Oh!
OH!
Oh!
Oooooooooooooooooh!

you're so quiet he says
you never used to be that quiet

nnoooooooooo
type my fingers against rock
I'm not quiet
u r not listening.

Sunday pm
Arianne knocks
go he says
I don't mind
before I reach the bedroom
clothes off
before I reach the front door
bathers on

I pause in my bolt
to say
bye back soon
slip into Arianne's car
soon
soon
we will slip into the sea

Out past the pontoon
Arianne holds my face
she strokes her fingers
down my cheek
then slaps me hard
I go under
snort salt water
my cheek and the back of my throat sting
is this supposed to help I say
work it out she says
she would slap me
as many times as it took
if she thought it would work
although I can see
the cost
of just one slap
in her face
I swim back
cold water fast breathing
reflection in car window
shows
my heated face
fingerprints
dulled to mottled apples
on my cheek

I think about it all the way home
glance in the rearview mirror
I try to look like I am not looking
surely her finger marks
blaze over my cheek
it's all right she says
there's no cosmetic damage
I know she's got a down
on Thistlehead
just what does she object to
I beat my fist against my thigh
I'm fighting with this I say

you feel anything like us
in chat
she says
I've loved her since
I was 11
I haven't known them as long I say
think again
she says
you'll never feel that in chat
never see my eyes fill
never taste our tears
in the ocean

this is what she believes
chat is fantasy
how many times
would she need to slap my face
before I believed it too

she won't be able to I know
one slap
all she can do
the nowords space
between the slap
and wishing
you never had.

This is the deal
I drop some chat
he reduces overtime
not too much
we circle around the house
the children bewildered
by our tracings
lines are softer
at the ocean
I take us all there
we can swim to the pontoon
talk about sharks
jump from the pontoon
into each other's arms
if I jump enough
water will get into my ears
at midnight
I'll already be asleep
I'll lie still in his bed, our bed
I won't need to fight
my fingers won't type
I'll be asleep
I can hardly walk to the car
or wash away salt
he massages my shoulders

as if he knows
muscles are tensed
to stop my fingers from typing
as if he knows it is impossible
but I have done it
for a day
we have done it for a day

We eat fish and chips
stuff more in
than is good
he doesn't make work calls
we talk with the children
make plans
for beach holidays
when we are lying in bed
it seems no hardship
to turn over
kiss him lips to lips
open my lips even
run my tongue inside his lower lip
this is no hardship I can do this
you don't have to he says
mmmm nor do you I say
our words coagulate
across the void
I think of nowords
the nowords space
between the tongue
inside the lower lip
and responding to desire
I do not fill the space with words.

Dogs have been known to die from eating a sea hare

I am in the sea
in waves near rocks
kelp is thick and sweeps my flesh
in and out swirling in the wash
the children ride their boards
down a chute of water
again and again

I look into pools
their edges fringed with black nerites
seaweed periwinkles barnacles
I peer further to fringes of anemones
brown black orange red
nodules of pink coral
juvenile fish sea slugs

I look through layers
encrusted lips
plunge in hands
reach jelly masses
that suck on my fingers

the dog has chewed the snorkels
so I dive and dive
with my goggles into the wash
peering into kelp
until I am breathless
but cannot stop
wanting to breathe underwater
gripping a piece of rock
limbs buffeted
looking for the red starfish
glimpses of red
beneath the kelp
I am breathless

we anoint our bodies
cover our heads
I lie on scorched sea rocks
with a hot sun above
a sandwich filling of cold air
blows across my belly

I wash dishes
outside in
a plastic sink
let chocolate melt
on my tongue
dribble down
my throat
all day I have
watched children
roll like dogs
in the sand
watched for
tiger snakes
march flies
mosquitoes
sea hares
king waves
I read love
in the time
of cholera
by gaslight
lick salt from
inside my lip

you move your
director's chair closer
your fingers
catch the nape
of my neck
in a half hurting
kind of a way
mmm I say
and do not flinch
my body is full
of the touch
of the ocean
if I concentrate
I can predict
your moves
pinch
my thigh
kiss
my inner arm
nuzzle
into my neck
a predicted touch
on my salted skin
is not so bad

at midnight I think of Thistlehead
compose my message to him
dogs have been known to die
from eating a sea hare
I cannot send it to him
I am getting away from it all
I have no electronic devices
I have not thought of
Thistlehead all day
or half the night
but at midnight, midnight,
I need to write
an email of the day
press send, send
to Thistlehead
but I have promised
I have no devices
no artifice
I try
try so hard
but my fingers type
against my thigh
brb brb brb
be right back.

Postscript

think of it then, think of nowords
find the space of nowords
a breath of nowords
refreshing, undemanding
can you find it there
between the break of one wave and the next?
it is the breath between words
or the eyescrinklesmile between friends
the slow pause
on the downsweep of tired eyelids
the moment between a baby's last suck
and the release of the nipple
but now I have told you these things
you will fill those spaces with words
ahh yes, you will say to yourself with words
this is the nowords space
of the eyescrinklesmile between friends
and you will have filled another nowords space
with words.

the end

References

Anonymous. "Love Poems". *The Penguin Book of Women Poets* Ed.Cosman, C. Keefe, J. & Weaver, K. Viking Press, 1979, New York.

Austen, J. *Pride and Prejudice*. Penguin English Library, Penguin UK, 2013, United Kingdom.

Blyton, E. *Five are Together Again*. 1st Edition, Hodder & Stoughton, 1963, Hachette, United Kingdom.

Falk, L. "Captain Amazon - Pirate Queen". *The Phantom*, Iss. 0958, Frew Publications, 1990, Sydney, Australia.

Fitzgerald, F. S. "The Great Gatsby". *The Collected Works of F. Scott Fitzgerald*, Wordsworth Special Editions, Wordsworth Editions Ltd, 2011, Hertfordshire, United Kingdom.

Noyes, A. "The Highwayman", *iF - A Treasury of Poems for Almost Every Possibility*, Ed. Esiri, A. & Kelly, R. Canongate Books, 2012, Edinburgh, United Kingdom.

Melville, H. *Moby Dick or, The Whale*, Marshall Cavendish, 1987, London, United Kingdom.

Neruda, P. "Tonight I can write", *The Picador Book of Love Poems*, Ed. Stammers, J. Picador Books, Pan MacMillan, 2012, London, United Kingdom.

Shakespeare, W. *The Sonnets*, Plume and Meridian Books, 1964 New York, USA.

Yeats, W. K. "Leda and the Swan", *Yeats*, Everyman's Library, David Campbell Pub Ltd, 1995, London, United Kingdom.

Acknowledgements

My appreciation and thanks to the Albany Writers Group especially Libby Corson, Barbara Temperton, Andrew Turke and Dianne Wolfer. Also thanks also to publisher and assistant publisher Bronwyn Mehan and Camilla Cripps, and editor Rhiannon Hall, at Spineless Wonders for their work with the manuscript and the whole digital and now print adventure.

About the Author

Maree Dawes is an Albany poet, published nationally and internationally. Maree's first collection *Women of the Minotaur* explored the lives of mistresses in Picasso's life. It was featured on Poetica in May 2009 and dramatised for the program launch for Perth International Arts Festival 2010. Her short story *I am so sweet and truthful* was also adapted into a short film. Maree has collaborated with artists, dancers and embroiderers.

About this Series

www.shortaustralianstories.com.au

Cover designs for the Spineless Wonders Small stories are by Bettina Kaiser.